BOLD:

TYPICALLY DESCRIBES ONE WHO IS WILLING TO TAKE RISKS; WHO IS BRAVE IN HEART AS WELL AS DEED

BOLD TALES FOR
BRAVE-HEARTED BOYS

SUSANNAH MCFARLANE

ALLEN&UNWIN
SYDNEY · MELBOURNE · AUCKLAND · LONDON

First published by Allen & Unwin in 2019

Allen & Unwin
83 Alexander Street
Crows Nest NSW 2065
Australia
Phone: (61 2) 8425 0100
Email: info@allenandunwin.com
Web: www.allenandunwin.com

A catalogue record for this book is available from the National Library of Australia

ISBN 978 1 76052 471 5

For teaching resources, explore www.allenandunwin.com/resources/for-teachers

Cover and text design by Sandra Nobes
Cover illustration: compilation by Sandra Nobes
Cover image silhouettes: giant © Brenton McKenna; Hansel, Gretel and witch © Simon Howe; thinking boy © Matt Huynh; dragons © Louie Joyce; birds © In Art & Bildagentur Zoonar GmbH / Shutterstock; additional images © Sandra Nobes / Allen & Unwin
Set in 15 pt Horley Old Style by Sandra Nobes
Printed and bound in June 2019 by C&C Offset Printing Co. Ltd., China

1 3 5 7 9 10 8 6 4 2

www.susannahmcfarlane.com
www.facebook.com/ubbysunderdogs
www.simonhowe.com.au
www.matthuynh.com
www.louiejoyce.com

Contents

PREFACE   VII

JACK AND THE BEANSTALK   1
illustrated by Brenton McKenna

HANSEL AND GRETEL   29
illustrated by Simon Howe

THE EMPEROR'S NEW CLOTHES 59
illustrated by Matt Huynh

PRINCE LEO AND THE
SLEEPING PRINCESS   89
illustrated by Louie Joyce

For Edvard,
the bravest, most bold-hearted boy I know,
with love and admiration

ONCE UPON A TIME, in a land far away
(yet not so different from today),
four young boys must show their best
to overcome an epic test.

Battles are fought and dragons slain;
evildoers kept from ill-gotten gain.
Yet our heroes find, as perhaps will you,
that it's how as well as what you do.

The boy who wins the battle well,
as these tales of courage tell,
may not be the biggest, nor play the largest part,
but be clever, honest and bold of heart.

For strong is more than muscle and might:
it's following your heart to do what's right.
Then boys, no matter how young or small,
can claim great victory and peace for all.

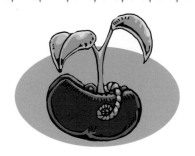

JACK AND THE BEANSTALK

I.

ONCE UPON A TIME in the Upper Lands, high in the sky, lived a boy called Jack. Jack was a good boy, gentle and helpful. Each morning, after taking tea and toast to his mother in bed, making sure the slices were spread with just the right amount of butter and jam, Jack would set off for the woods. There he'd uproot pine trees, to be made into furniture in a nearby village called the Tablelands. For Jack, or Gentle Jack, or GJ as his mother and pretty much everyone in the villages called him, was a giant, and pulling up the tall trees was the perfect job for him.

No one was sure why GJ was a giant, he just was – and, as it happened, his size was just what was needed for his special job. In fact, everyone in the Upper Lands had their own special job to do, needing their exact special talent.

1

Each time GJ pulled up a tree in the woods, he'd take a pine seed from his large pocket and plant it in the hole left behind. Everything grew quickly in the Upper Lands, nourished by the silver rain that fell from the sky, and in just weeks a new tree would be ready to be harvested. Despite having enormous fingers, GJ was very careful to place each tiny seed in exactly the right place, spreading just the right amount of dirt over it, grinning as the first green shoots popped up immediately.

GJ was happy in his work, and because he was also a creative boy, he liked making up little chants as he walked, pulled and planted.

Hey, ho, hi, hum,
heave the trees, up they come!
Drop the seed, wait a mo',
see the tree begin to grow!

GJ stacked his trees against a huge boulder in a big clearing, one atop another. When he'd stacked fifty trees, it'd be time for his favourite part of the job: tree-snagging. GJ had developed his very own tree-snagging technique, lassoing the trees together with a long, long rope. Each time, he'd test

himself by trying to do this from further away from the stack.
Now GJ could snag the pile and haul it towards him from a
mile away, an amazing record for even a boy of GJ's size.

GJ would then haul the wood to the Tablelands, where
the villagers milled it and crafted it into beautiful tables and
chairs.

'Great bundle today, big guy,' called the Mayor of the
Tablelands one morning as GJ arrived.

'Thank you, sir,' replied GJ, beaming. 'Oh, and here's
your egg.' He took a gleaming golden egg from his shirt

pocket and handed it
to the Mayor.

That was
another special
thing about GJ.
On the day he
was born, a white
goose walked into his mother's farmhouse. That would have
been strange enough, but even stranger was that this goose
laid golden eggs, one every day.

'It was a day of double blessing,' GJ's mother always said.
'Precious eggs and an even more precious
boy with a heart so
big it needed the body
of a giant to hold it!'

And so, each day,
when he delivered
the wood, Jack also
brought an egg. A
villager would carry
it off to the smelter,
where it would be melted

down into gold coins and shared among all who lived in the Upper Lands.

'Thank you, GJ,' said the Mayor, 'and here are some coins for you and your mother.'

As he spoke, a team of villagers arrived with a very tall ladder. GJ knelt down and they leant the ladder against him. Then one of the villagers climbed up and handed him a bulging cloth sack.

'There's a bit more today so you can buy materials for your project,' she said. 'And we've popped in one of your favourite lollies. The sweet-maker spent all day spinning the sugar for you.'

GJ's smile grew wider as he took out a huge red-and-yellow-striped whopper-sucker all-day lollipop.

'Thank you, everyone,' he cried. 'Delicious! And that's exactly how many coins I need to buy the metal for my Incredible Flower-pulling Machine!'

'Our pleasure, GJ. You deserve it,' said the Mayor.

As he walked home, GJ sucked on his lollipop and thought about the metal he'd buy at the Ironlands the next day after he'd finished work. While GJ was the perfect boy for picking trees, picking the tiny, delicate flowers his mother liked in her tea was tricky for him. The contraption he'd designed would be just the thing for that.

That evening, over dinner, GJ told his mother about his day and his plans for the Incredible Flower-pulling Machine. After stacking the plates in the dish-scrubbing box he'd invented, leaving the coins on the table ready for the following day, GJ helped his mother into bed, brought her a cup of tea, made sure she was comfortable and leant down, down, down to kiss her goodnight.

'You're a good son, GJ,' she said, kissing the top of his giant nose. 'And remember, when in doubt...'

'Do good,' said GJ.

'Exactly,' replied his mother. 'Sleep well, my giant-hearted boy.'

GJ smiled and tiptoed out, leaving her door slightly ajar so she'd hear the beautiful lullabies their magical golden harp, a gift from the villagers, would play for them throughout the night.

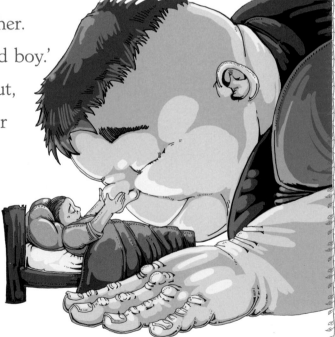

But that night, lying in his giant bed, GJ had to strain to hear his harp above the sounds of some angry voices floating up from the Lower Lands below him.

'Foolish boy, you gave our last cow to someone for five beans? *Beans?* What were you thinking?' snapped a woman's voice.

'But, Mother,' a boy's voice cried, 'the man said they were magic! And it would have taken so long to walk the cow all the way to the market.'

'Lazy, disobedient boy!' replied the mother. 'Magic? Honestly, Jack, how could you be so stupid?'

Another Jack? thought GJ. *He may have the same name as me but my mother and I don't argue like that.*

Below in the Lower Lands, a door slammed and the voices finally quietened, so that GJ could hear the harp's soothing lullaby again.

'Thank goodness,' he murmured as his eyelids started drooping. In seconds, the giant boy was asleep and all was peaceful and calm in the Upper Lands.

2.

THAT NIGHT, as everyone in both lands slept, something strange was happening in the Lower Lands. Jack's mother had thrown the beans her son had brought home out the kitchen door in disgust, slamming it shut after them. The beans had landed in an unused vegetable plot, and now a beanstalk took root and began to grow… fast. It grew higher than the weeds and thistles. It grew higher than the farmhouse and all the surrounding trees.

In fact, it grew higher than everything in the Lower Lands, and by the next morning it had grown right up through the clouds into the Upper Lands.

But when GJ headed off to work the next morning, he knew none of this. He didn't see the beanstalk, nor the very small boy hauling himself up it, through the swirling, misty cloud mantle.

That small boy was the Lower Lands Jack, who now stood in the Upper Lands. In the distance, he could see a house.

Hmmm, worth a look, thought Jack. *You never know your luck.* As Jack got closer to the house, he realised it was tall – very tall. *A giant must live here*, he thought as he reached the door. *It would take at least twenty of me to even reach the keyhole! Maybe the giant has treasure!*

To Jack's surprise, the door was open. (For there was no need to lock doors in the Upper Lands.) He went inside and found himself in a kitchen with a fireplace, a very high table, one very large low chair, and one very small high chair.

Definitely a giant, decided Jack, climbing up a long coil of rope hanging from the high table. 'My!' he cried as he stepped onto the table and spied the coins, which GJ had forgotten to take with him that morning. 'Treasure! This is indeed my lucky day.

And I deserve these coins. I'm sure whoever lives here doesn't need them half as much as I do. I might even give my mother some, if she's lucky.'

'Is there someone out there?' came a thin voice from another room, making Jack jump with fright. It was GJ's mother.

Then, much to his surprise, music began to play. Jack spun around, knocking over a sugar bowl on the table, to see a golden harp by the fireplace playing music – alarmingly loud music, all by itself.

Next, the house began to shake. 'This house is enchanted!' cried Jack, and he ran across the table, leaving little boot prints in the sugar. He snatched the sack of coins and slid back down the rope to the kitchen floor.

The house was shaking because GJ was running towards it. He'd not gone far from home when his nose had begun to twitch – for Upper Landers had an exceptional sense of smell.

Fee, fi, fo, fum,
I smell the scent of a Lower Lands man.
I will rush so I can see
who this Lower Lander might be!

And so GJ had run towards the smell. It wasn't often that visitors made their way to the Upper Lands, and GJ was eager to learn how the stranger had got there. He was a little surprised, however, when he realised he was running in the direction of his own house. His surprise turned to fear when he heard his harp wailing, and he ran faster and harder, his steps now thundering on the ground.

Jack, meanwhile, looked longingly at the golden harp by the fireplace, but he knew he had no time to lose and he dashed out the door towards the beanstalk. By the time GJ reached home, Jack was back in the Lower Lands.

GJ rushed in the front door. He saw the overturned bowl and the tiny boot prints in the sugar on the table, and realised with consternation that the sack of gold coins was gone. Whoever would take something that didn't belong to them? That simply didn't happen in the Upper Lands.

'GJ, is that you?' came his mother's voice.

'Mum!' he cried, rushing into her room. 'Are you all right?'

GJ was so relieved his mother was unharmed that he burst into tears and all but forgot about the coins. His mum gave his cheek a big hug and wiped his tears away, which made GJ feel a lot better – but what on earth, they wondered, was going on?

3.

THE NEXT MORNING, GJ didn't want to leave his mother, but she insisted. 'You must do your work, GJ,' she said gently. 'The Tablelands depend on you.'

So GJ set off reluctantly, sad he no longer had the coins to buy iron for his machine, and worried about his mum.

> *Bish, bash, bo, bum,*
> *I am feeling a little glum...*

GJ chanted with less than his usual vigour as he walked the path to the woods. Once he reached the woods, however, and could breathe the fresh air and hear the chirping, buzzing, busy noises of the woodland animals, GJ quickly cheered up and set to work.

Meanwhile, down in the Lower Lands, Jack was setting off up the beanstalk again, a large empty sack on his back. He planned to steal the golden harp, for it would fetch a pretty penny at the markets. So off he went, through the cloud mantle again and into GJ's house.

Jack was relieved to hear snoring coming from the bedroom this time. He tiptoed towards the hearth where, as he'd hoped, he saw the harp – and, to his surprise, a goose sitting in a wooden box.

'Hello, my pretty,' he whispered.
'I didn't notice you last time. You
look good and plump; you'll make
a nice Sunday dinner, for sure.
I'll take you too.'

Jack picked up the goose only
to jump back in surprise and delight:
there in the box was a large golden egg.

'Yes!' hissed Jack. 'I'll never have to work again! The giant
must have hundreds of eggs and doesn't need any more –
and I most certainly do!' And he greedily stuffed the harp
and the goose and the golden egg into his sack, the cloth
muffling the noise of the harp.

'The sooner I melt you into gold the better,' he said,
tying up the sack. Then
he threw it over his
shoulder and ran out
of the house towards
the beanstalk.

In the forest, GJ got the twitching feeling in his nose again.

Fee, fi, fo, fum,
I smell the scent of that Lower Lands man.

GJ took off, running as fast as he could. This time, the scent led him to the very edge of the Upper Lands, where he saw the top tendrils of the beanstalk. Peering through the cloud mantle, he saw the enormous beanstalk twisting downwards and could just make out a small boy far below.

GJ wasted no time. He leapt onto the beanstalk and clambered after the boy. With his long legs, he soon caught up. He plucked the boy from the stalk.

'Oi!' cried the boy. GJ dangled him in front of his face, studying him. 'What are you doing?' yelled the boy crossly.

'What am I doing?' asked GJ. 'What are *you* doing? You're Jack, aren't you?'

'What's it to you?' snapped the boy. 'Put me down!'

Just then, a muffled *honk* came from the sack over Jack's back, followed by a frantic-sounding harp melody. Realising that this boy surely had stolen his coins the day before, and was now bold enough to have stolen both his family's beautiful harp *and* their beloved goose, GJ began to feel very, very cross indeed.

He pinched the boy a little more tightly, and Jack realised he was in no position to make demands of this giant.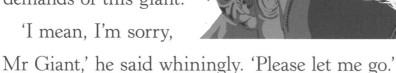

'I mean, I'm sorry, Mr Giant,' he said whiningly. 'Please let me go.'

'Did you take my coins yesterday?'

'No,' said Jack, gulping.

GJ pulled Jack even closer towards him. He wanted to see his eyes more closely, for he wasn't at all sure he believed him. Jack, however, thought the giant was about to eat him, so he changed his story.

'Yes!' he cried. 'I mean yes! I am sorry, truly! I only did it because we're so poor, and I wanted to help my old, sick – very, very sick – mother. I was doing it for her. Please don't hurt me. I'll never steal again, I promise. Please, kind sir, I beg you, don't eat me.'

GJ was taken aback – he had no idea why Jack thought

he would eat him – but Jack's talk of helping his mother had made GJ feel less cross towards him. Perhaps Jack needed the coins more than he did. Perhaps this was his chance to do some good?

'Hmm,' said GJ, not realising that a giant *hmmm* can sound rather frightening if you aren't used to hearing it.

'Please!' shrieked Jack. 'I'll do anything!'

'Okay,' said GJ, plucking the sack from the boy's back. 'I want my harp and my goose back, but you can keep the egg, for your mother.'

'What?' said Jack. *Why would he do that?* he wondered.

'You heard me – keep the egg,' said GJ, putting Jack back on a lower branch of the beanstalk. 'But keep your promise, never steal again – and never come to the Upper Lands again, either.'

Jack scampered down the beanstalk without so much as a thankyou to GJ. *I don't want that lump changing his mind about that golden egg and coming down after me*, he thought as he reached the ground. *I'll chop down the beanstalk.* And he grabbed the axe from the pile of unchopped wood in his yard and started hacking at the base of the stalk.

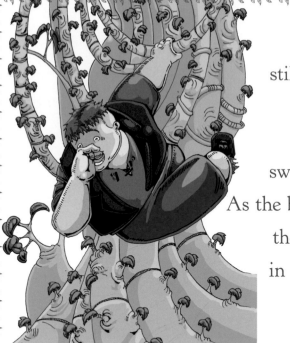

'Hey!' shouted GJ, who was still halfway up it. 'Stop it, or the beanstalk will fall and I'll die!'

'Not my problem!' cried Jack, swinging the axe again and again. As the beanstalk wobbled, GJ dropped the sack with the harp and goose in it and it fell and caught on one of the beanstalk's lower shoots. GJ had to get his goose back – the villagers would be lost without its eggs – but the beanstalk was getting wobblier and wobblier. GJ was scared. He didn't want to fall. He looked up: he could retreat home, where he'd be safe, but then what about the goose? GJ took a giant breath and started climbing downwards instead.

Jack had also seen the sack drop, and now he raced up the beanstalk, greed overtaking him. 'Stupid, clumsy giant,' he cried, 'I'll have my harp and goose after all.'

Jack was nimbler than GJ, and he reached the sack first, snatching it and beginning to climb back down. But GJ had an idea. He uncoiled his tree-snagging rope, looked directly at the sack, swung the rope down and snagged the sack! Then he started climbing for home, the sack trailing after him.

'Hey!' shouted Jack, 'you can't! It's mine!'

'No, it's not,' called GJ over his shoulder.

Rage overtook Jack. As GJ hauled himself safely back to the Upper Lands, panting in relief, Jack began climbing after GJ up the now very wobbly beanstalk.

Then, from below, GJ heard a cry: 'Help, help! I'm stuck and the beanstalk is about to fall!' It was coming from down the beanstalk. It was Jack.

GJ was horrified. *Jack will surely die*, he thought. *But if I try to help him, so might I. And he treated me really badly.*

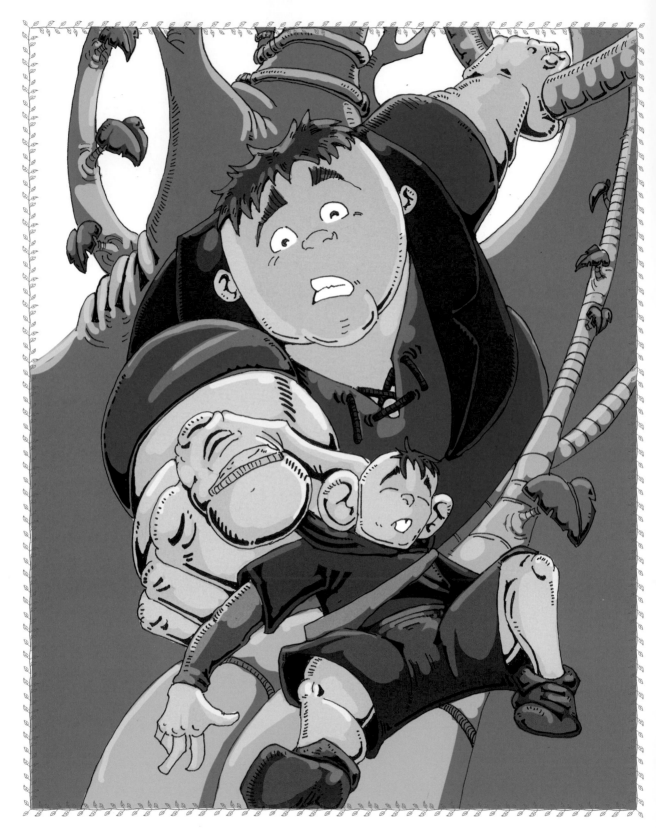

'Help!'

GJ knew he couldn't stand by and let Jack die, no matter how badly he'd behaved – he had to do the right thing and help. He climbed back onto the beanstalk. The wind blew strongly, and the beanstalk swung terribly from side to side, but GJ carried on until he found Jack tangled in a broken beanstalk tendril.

Crack!

The beanstalk lurched to one side. *It's starting to fall!* GJ realised. He plucked up Jack, who fainted in shock. GJ put him in his pocket. Then he pushed on down the beanstalk, dropped the boy onto a soft haystack, and climbed back upwards as fast as he could.

Crack!

The beanstalk lurched again. There were more cracks and groans as huge tendrils began to fall around him.

GJ pushed on and up. He was nearly there. If he could just—

Crack!

With that last crack Jack woke up, in time to see the beanstalk crash to earth.

Had the giant who'd saved his life made it back to the Upper Lands? Jack didn't know.

26

4.

ONE BRIGHT MORNING just a few days later, after making his mother toast and tea in bed, Jack was up early. He'd spent the past days cleaning away the beanstalk branches and tending to the vegetable garden. He'd decided he'd like to grow food for himself and his mother.

Jack was taking a break when, on the front step, he saw a small box attached to a parachute. He removed the strings and opened the box. Inside were three golden eggs. A huge smile broke across Jack's face. This could only be

from the giant. He'd made it back up to the Upper Lands –
he was safe! He must have made that clever parachute, too.

Jack looked down again at the eggs and, as tears pricked
his eyes, he felt something he hadn't felt before. 'Why would
he do that? For me, who stole from him?' he whispered
aloud. 'I don't deserve this.' He looked up at the clear blue
sky above. 'Thank you,' he said. 'I'll do something really
good with them. I promise.'

And he did – and both Jacks and their families lived
happily ever after.

HANSEL AND GRETEL

I.

ONCE UPON A TIME, in a land ravaged by failing crops and famine, lived twins called Hansel and Gretel. A spell had been cast over the land, hardening the ground and the hearts of those who tried to till it. Disease was rife, and the twins' parents were taken by illness, leaving them to the reluctant charity of their uncle and aunt, who lived in a small cottage on the edge of a large wood.

The aunt and uncle toiled hard each day. They chopped firewood to sell in the village, but no one had money to spare. Often the most they'd manage to exchange before the long walk home were a few stale buns and a bag of flour. At home, they'd mix the flour sparingly with water to make bread and, using the leaves of the few stunted cabbages that managed to grow, boil a watery soup. But none of it was ever enough to fill their stomachs, and the poor family groaned with hunger from morning until night.

'What will become of us?' wailed the aunt to her husband. 'Soon winter will come, and we'll not even have these cabbages to eat. We can barely feed ourselves, let alone your poor dead brother's children. This can't go on!'

Hansel and Gretel tried to help. Gretel, who was strong and loved to be outside, helped chop wood while Hansel, who wasn't so strong but was exceptionally good at solving puzzles, ordered the logs in perfect piles outside the kitchen. Gretel stoked the fire with the heavy metal poker, while Hansel carefully measured out flour and water, using as little as possible to make the most bread.

But there was never enough food.

'How will we survive?' lamented the aunt, stirring the watery soup. 'We'll surely starve!'

Each night Hansel and Gretel climbed up to their straw mattress in the attic. Lying side by side, they'd tell each other stories to take their minds off their rumbling stomachs.

Gretel made up stories of great adventure, in which she'd rescue someone – usually Hansel – from ravenous wolves in the woods, or eye-pecking birds that swooped down from the sky. Gretel's eyes always shone as she told these stories. Hansel would often interrupt to ask the details: How many wolves were there? How big were the ravens?

Other times, Hansel told
Gretel instead how one day
they'd have a little shop, where they'd
make and sell all manner of delicious
things that for now, huddled in their straw
bed, they could only dream of: gingerbread
biscuits, candy-striped lollipops and soft-centred caramels
that people would come from far and wide to buy.

Then the twins would snuggle into each other and, their
breathing falling into the same rhythm, they'd sleep until
their hunger pains woke them the next morning.

One moon-bright autumn night Hansel and Gretel heard their uncle and aunt talking in hushed tones downstairs.

'This can't go on, I tell you,' said the aunt. 'We will all surely die!'

'The children are of little help,' said the uncle, 'yet they have hungry stomachs to fill.'

The twins looked at each other sadly. Then the voices below became lower still, and they couldn't make out the words, until they heard their uncle say at last: 'It's decided.'

'It's the only way,' agreed the aunt. 'And, after all, they are not our children.'

'Tomorrow, first thing,' said the uncle, 'I'll tell them we need to chop wood, take them deep into the forest and leave them there.'

Hansel and Gretel were horrified, for they'd heard of the witches and wolves that stalked the deep woods. No one dared go in, not even to find the sweet berries said to grow there.

'I'll stop this, Hansel!' whispered Gretel fiercely. 'I'll go down and tell them—'

'No, sister,' said Hansel, 'we need a plan, to show them we can be useful.'

'True, brother,' replied Gretel. 'But how?'

'If we go into the woods,' replied Hansel, looking out the attic window to the moonlit yard below, 'we can collect berries for us all to eat.'

Gretel thought of the wolves, then squared her shoulders. 'I can carry lots,' she said. 'But how will we get home?'

Hansel furrowed his brow, a sign he was thinking. He was looking at some white stones in the yard, gleaming in the moonlight.

'We'll make a trail to lead us back,' he said, 'with those white stones. We need to collect them now – but how do we get down there without Uncle and Aunt seeing?'

'Leave that to me,' said Gretel with a glint in her eyes.

Gretel ran to the window and shimmied down the cottage wall. She stuffed stones into the large pockets of her grubby pinafore, climbed back up, and emptied the pile of stones onto their bed not three minutes later.

'You did it!' said Hansel.

'We did it,' replied Gretel, grinning. They put their thumbs together in their secret handshake and, as they snuggled back into bed, Hansel told Gretel the rest of his plan.

2.

THE NEXT MORNING, as the cockerel crowed, the uncle called gruffly: 'Come down, children. We have work to do in the woods.'

Hansel and Gretel looked at each other, put their thumbs together and nodded. Then Hansel filled his pockets with the white stones and they climbed down the ladder into the kitchen.

'Ready, Uncle,' they said.

'Here,' said the wife curtly. 'A crust of bread each for the way.'

The three set off into the woods in silence, chewing their crusts, trying to make each mouthful last as long as it could. Hansel dropped white stones at regular intervals.

Deep in the woods, the uncle
stopped. 'Wait here, children. I'll
chop wood then fetch you to help carry it.'
'Yes, Uncle,' replied Hansel and Gretel,
but they knew he was lying. He walked away, looking
back only once at the two children in the dark woods.

When he was gone, Hansel said, 'Now for our plan, sister.
We'll collect more berries in one day than we've had
all autumn. When we return, Uncle and Aunt
will be so happy they'll allow us to stay.'
Indeed, there were many more ripe, juicy
berries growing in these woods than at the
cottage. Gretel, being faster and
stronger, collected the most, but
Hansel checked them all, making
sure none were rotten.
As the day neared its
end, their pockets bulged.
Now they turned towards
home, eyes on the
ground, looking
for the white stones.

Gretel ran ahead, calling back to her brother: 'Here's one, Hansel! Here's another! Your plan worked – you did it!'

'We did it,' replied her brother.

Gretel waited patiently as Hansel caught up with her before dashing ahead again... and it was nearly dark when they reached the cottage and burst through the kitchen door.

'Look, Uncle! Look, Aunt!' cried Gretel.

'We have berries!' cried Hansel.

But their aunt and uncle only stared at them and then each other, not even noticing the berries bulging in the children's pockets. Hansel and Gretel watched, crestfallen, as the adults whispered. Then the uncle said harshly to the children: 'Did I not tell you to wait in the woods?'

'Yes, Uncle,' said Gretel, 'but—'

'Are the berries to make up for disobedience?' asked the aunt sharply.

'We'll return to the woods. Now,' said the uncle. 'You'll do as I say.'

Hansel and Gretel were alarmed. There was no time to collect more stones. What would they do?

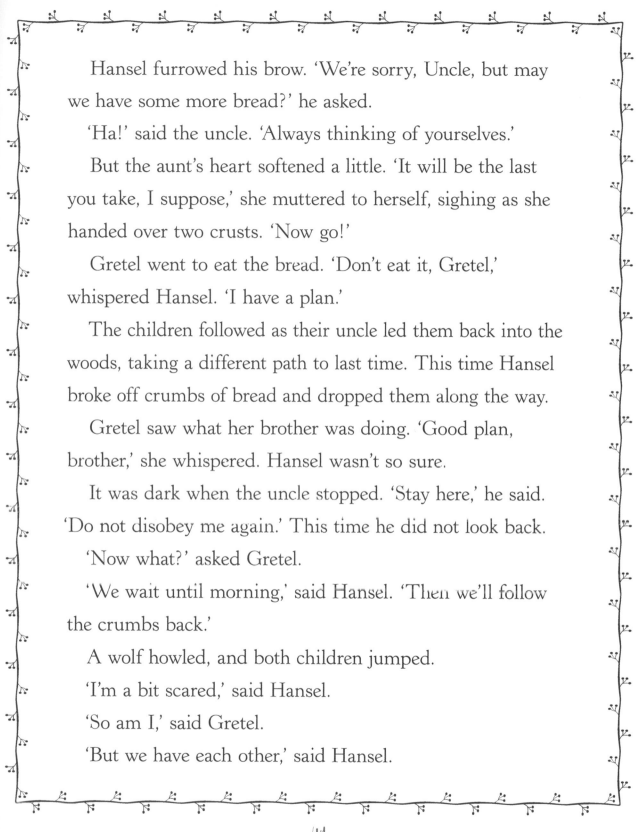

Hansel furrowed his brow. 'We're sorry, Uncle, but may we have some more bread?' he asked.

'Ha!' said the uncle. 'Always thinking of yourselves.'

But the aunt's heart softened a little. 'It will be the last you take, I suppose,' she muttered to herself, sighing as she handed over two crusts. 'Now go!'

Gretel went to eat the bread. 'Don't eat it, Gretel,' whispered Hansel. 'I have a plan.'

The children followed as their uncle led them back into the woods, taking a different path to last time. This time Hansel broke off crumbs of bread and dropped them along the way.

Gretel saw what her brother was doing. 'Good plan, brother,' she whispered. Hansel wasn't so sure.

It was dark when the uncle stopped. 'Stay here,' he said. 'Do not disobey me again.' This time he did not look back.

'Now what?' asked Gretel.

'We wait until morning,' said Hansel. 'Then we'll follow the crumbs back.'

A wolf howled, and both children jumped.

'I'm a bit scared,' said Hansel.

'So am I,' said Gretel.

'But we have each other,' said Hansel.

'Yes,' said Gretel.

And the two children smiled, put their thumbs together and nodded.

'Look, Hansel,' cried Gretel, 'I can gather up the fallen leaves to keep us warm.'

While his sister scooped up the leaves, Hansel found a sheltered spot under a large oak tree. The twins snuggled into each other and ate their berries for dinner. Then, with their blanket of leaves offering some comfort from the cold night air, they fell asleep.

3.

THE CHILDREN WOKE to sunbeams pushing through the forest trees and ants crawling across their legs and arms.

Gretel leapt up, stamping her feet furiously. 'That will only make them angry,' advised Hansel softly. 'Let's go home.'

'Yes,' cried Gretel, running ahead, searching for the crumbs. But she couldn't find a single one.

'None here, Hansel!' she cried, again and again. Finally she spotted one, but a black raven swooped down, screeching, and picked it up in its beak.

'Birds have eaten all the crumbs,' said Hansel. 'I should have thought of that. We're lost!'

'But we have each other,' said Gretel.

'Yes,' said Hansel, managing a little smile, 'but we are still lost.'

'I can choose the clearest path for us,' said Gretel. 'Come on, brother.'

And so the children walked on deeper into the woods, Gretel thrashing at the undergrowth when it blocked their path, using a large stick she'd found. Hansel, meanwhile, pointed out the odd dangerous insect and poisonous plant they needed to avoid. Between them they managed to walk quite some way, avoiding the stinging nettles and biting ants of the wood. After some hours they came to a clearing. At its far end, they saw a cottage.

'Perhaps whoever lives there might give us something to eat,' said Gretel and ran ahead. When she got closer, she turned back. 'Oh quick, Hansel,' she shouted. 'Come quickly. You'll never believe this!'

Indeed, the cottage was no ordinary cottage. While it had a door with two windows either side and a roof, as most cottages do, this cottage wasn't made of stone, nor wood nor thatching. Instead, it was made entirely of things one could eat – mouth-wateringly sweet things Hansel and Gretel had

never dreamt of seeing, let alone eating. The walls were made of gingerbread, with pink-and-white icing piped up and down. Inlaid in the icing were marshmallows and boiled lollies – blue, yellow, red and purple. Licorice straps lined the window frames, and the windowsills held tiny cupcakes with lashings of frosted icing in all the colours of the rainbow. Jelly-chews formed heart shapes on the shutters. A little fence of candy canes circled the cottage, and fairy-floss flowers on

toffee stems stood in gingerbread flowerpots by the door.

To the side of the cottage was a vegetable patch, but sprouting from the soil of grated chocolate were even more lollies: caramel popcorn grew in clusters on a honeycomb-trellised vine of peppermint jelly leaves; boiled lollies as big as pumpkins grew from sprawling green licorice roots;

46

strawberry sherbet bombs burst from white chocolate flowers; and heads of soft jelly-drops grew like broccoli on thick stalks of green marzipan. Next to the patch, lemon-drop and toffee-apple tree branches bent over from the abundance of lolly-fruit on them.

Hansel and Gretel couldn't believe their eyes – or their noses. They licked their lips and gazed about in wonder.

'We have to try some, Gretel,' said Hansel, carefully removing a candy cane from the path and giving it a huge lick. 'Oh, it's delicious!'

Gretel took a cupcake from a windowsill and took a large bite. Jam oozed out of the cake, mingling deliciously in her mouth with the frosted icing. 'Hansel!' she exclaimed. 'Can this be real?'

But it was real, and soon the starving children were trying everything they could reach, filling their stomachs with pop-candies and lollipops, caramel-filled chocolates and strawberry marshmallows.

There was a creak as the front door opened. An old, shaky-sounding voice came from inside. 'Nibble, nibble, like a mouse. Is someone nibbling at my house?'

Hansel and Gretel jumped back, mouths full, as an old woman hobbled outside. She was dressed in a long black dress with a frilly white collar, and a red apron embroidered with little white hearts. She leant heavily on a wooden cane.

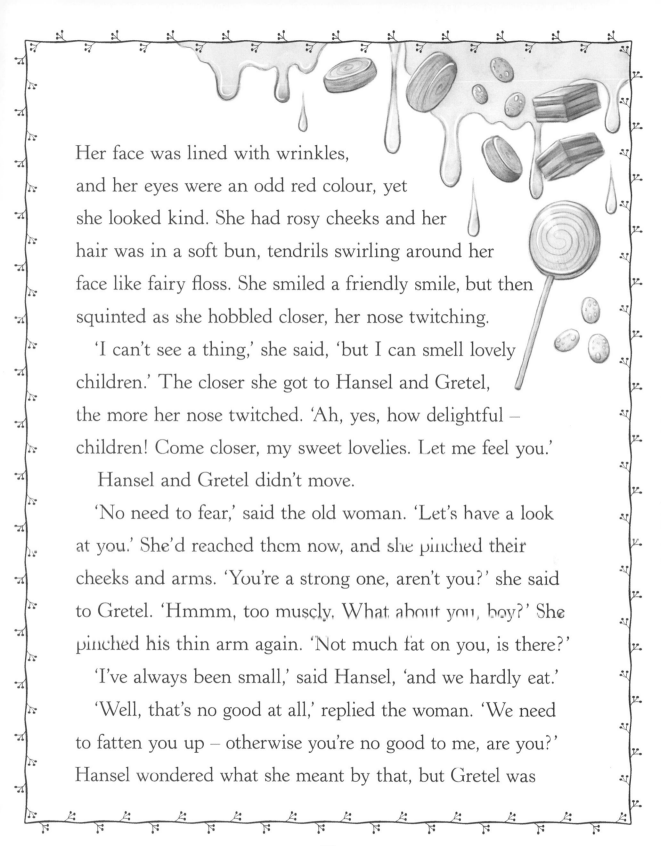

Her face was lined with wrinkles, and her eyes were an odd red colour, yet she looked kind. She had rosy cheeks and her hair was in a soft bun, tendrils swirling around her face like fairy floss. She smiled a friendly smile, but then squinted as she hobbled closer, her nose twitching.

'I can't see a thing,' she said, 'but I can smell lovely children.' The closer she got to Hansel and Gretel, the more her nose twitched. 'Ah, yes, how delightful – children! Come closer, my sweet lovelies. Let me feel you.'

Hansel and Gretel didn't move.

'No need to fear,' said the old woman. 'Let's have a look at you.' She'd reached them now, and she pinched their cheeks and arms. 'You're a strong one, aren't you?' she said to Gretel. 'Hmmm, too muscly. What about you, boy?' She pinched his thin arm again. 'Not much fat on you, is there?'

'I've always been small,' said Hansel, 'and we hardly eat.'

'Well, that's no good at all,' replied the woman. 'We need to fatten you up – otherwise you're no good to me, are you?' Hansel wondered what she meant by that, but Gretel was already chewing on a caramel the old woman had pushed into her mouth. 'Now, do come inside, my sweeties, and I'll make you each a large mug of hot chocolate with marshmallows.'

Hansel and Gretel looked at each other and nodded. If the old woman had made such delicious sweets, surely she was kind. 'Thank you!' they said, following her into the house.

As they entered, though, the door slammed shut behind them, and when the old woman turned back her face had changed. Her mouth had twisted into a mean snarl, and her red eyes flashed.

'You, my dears, are good enough to eat,' she said with a thin laugh, 'or at least you, boy, will be once I fatten you up!'

The children realised the old woman was a witch and had used her magical house to lure them in, but it was too late to escape. The door was locked, and as the witch banged her cane three times on the floor an iron cage fell down, imprisoning Hansel. Gretel pulled at the cage bars.

'Stop it, girl! Save your strength for chopping my wood, stirring my batter and feeding your brother.'

'No!' cried Gretel, pulling harder at the bars.

'There's no escape,' the witch said simply. 'You'll do as I say. I may not be much for seeing, but I can smell you perfectly. One move I don't command and your brother will be baked.'

Hansel and Gretel shook with fear. They were trapped.

4.

AND SO HANSEL was locked
in the spell-bound cage, and Gretel
was forced to work for the witch,
chopping wood in the wood room,
stirring the large vat of gingerbread
batter and feeding her brother plate
after plate of sweet food. What once
Hansel had dreamt of, now he dreaded:
cakes laden with cream, bowls of lollies and iced gingerbread.

'Getting fatter, soon to batter,' the witch repeated each
morning as she inspected Hansel to see how his plumping
had progressed. Unable to see properly, she'd pull out his
finger and feel it. 'Too skinny! More food!' she'd cackle.
'Once you're fat enough, I'll batter you up and bake you into
a gingerbread boy for my dinner.'

'No!' cried Gretel this particular morning.

'Disobey me and your brother will die sooner,' hissed the
witch. 'Do as I say and you'll have more time together.'

'Time,' said Hansel to himself, furrowing his brow.

'Gretel,' he whispered that night as she fed him cream cakes, 'when you're in the wood room, fetch me the thinnest stick you can find.'

'Yes, brother,' said Gretel, realising her brother had a plan. And the children smiled at each other, put their thumbs together and nodded.

Gretel slipped Hansel a thin stick, and the next morning he presented that to the witch rather than his finger, which indeed was getting plumper.

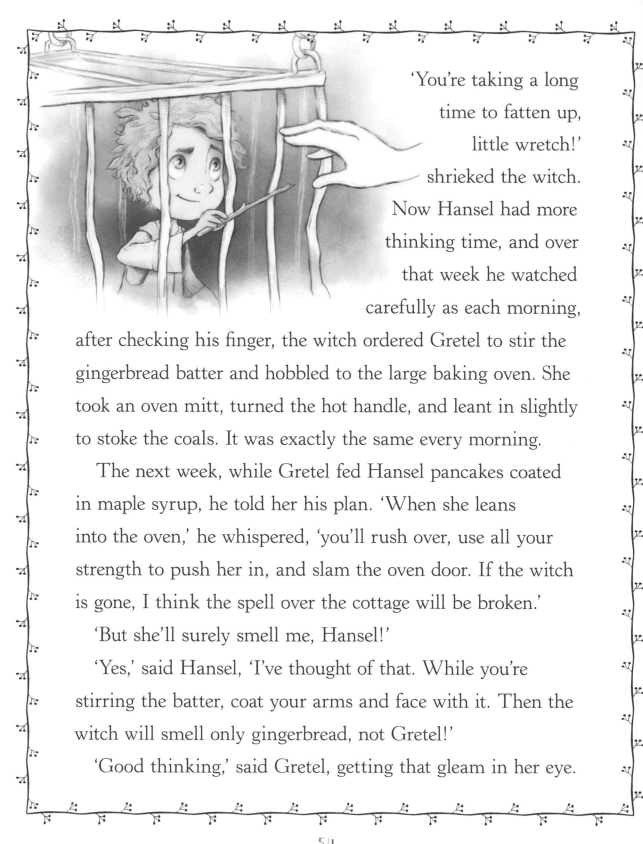

'You're taking a long time to fatten up, little wretch!' shrieked the witch. Now Hansel had more thinking time, and over that week he watched carefully as each morning, after checking his finger, the witch ordered Gretel to stir the gingerbread batter and hobbled to the large baking oven. She took an oven mitt, turned the hot handle, and leant in slightly to stoke the coals. It was exactly the same every morning.

The next week, while Gretel fed Hansel pancakes coated in maple syrup, he told her his plan. 'When she leans into the oven,' he whispered, 'you'll rush over, use all your strength to push her in, and slam the oven door. If the witch is gone, I think the spell over the cottage will be broken.'

'But she'll surely smell me, Hansel!'

'Yes,' said Hansel, 'I've thought of that. While you're stirring the batter, coat your arms and face with it. Then the witch will smell only gingerbread, not Gretel!'

'Good thinking,' said Gretel, getting that gleam in her eye.

'But, Gretel,' said Hansel, 'you will have to be quick.'

'I can do that,' said Gretel.

'And you will have to be strong.'

'I can do that too,' said Gretel.

'And you will have to be brave.'

Hansel saw his sister's lip quiver.

'You can do that, Gretel,' he said.

Gretel smiled, and they put their thumbs together and nodded.

The next morning, it happened just as Hansel had foretold. The witch checked Hansel's finger and crossly ordered Gretel to stir the batter. She then hobbled to the fire, leant into the oven and began stoking the coals.

Gretel moved like lightning. The witch's nose didn't even twitch; she never knew Gretel was coming. Gretel pushed the evil witch into the oven and, although the handle was scalding hot on her hand, slammed the door shut behind her.

The moment the door locked shut, the bars of Hansel's cage fell to the ground. The witch's spell had been broken.

'You did it, Gretel!' cried Hansel.

'We did it, Hansel!' cried Gretel.

The children hugged.

'What shall we do now, brother?' asked Gretel.

'I think I have a plan,' said Hansel.

'Of course you do,' said Gretel, hugging her dear brother again. 'Tell me all about it.'

5.

THE DEATH OF the witch had also broken the famine that blighted the land. The ground was softened by cleansing rains and, by spring, crops flourished and food was plentiful.

Hansel and Gretel lived in the cottage, no longer made of gingerbread but a strong and sturdy brick. They'd strung a large banner above the door: 'H&G Sweet Things Emporium and Inventions Workshop'.

The emporium sold all sort of lollies and gingerbreads and a few other things Hansel had created in his workshop –

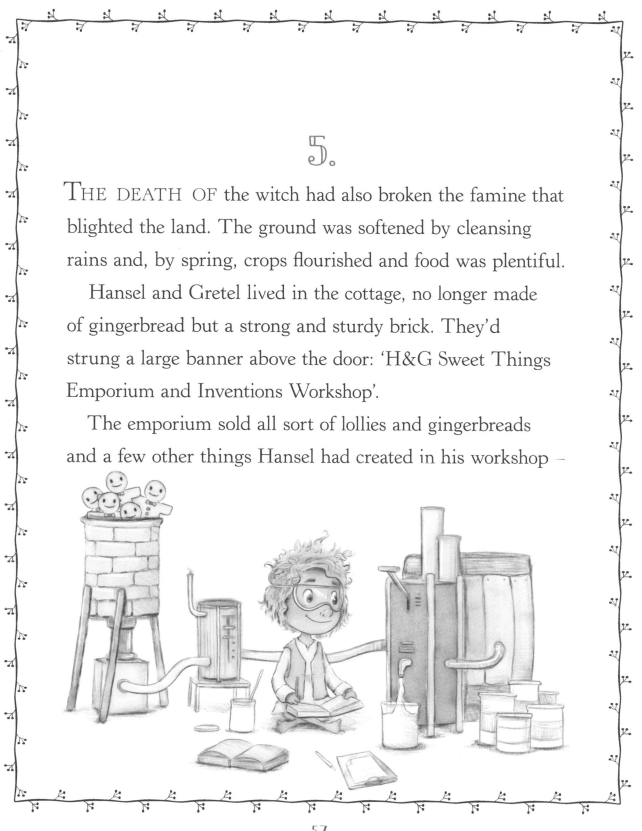

including his first invention, the Gingerbread Batter Burn Balm, a soothing cream that had healed Gretel's hand.

The vegetable patch now burst with an abundance of strawberries and grapes, pumpkins, sweetcorn, beans and broccoli, and Hansel, who had rather lost his sweet tooth, would crunch on cucumbers morning to night.

People came from all over to try the mouthwatering sweets and salads, paying as little or as much as they could afford. Everyone lived happily ever after – and nobody's stomach ever grumbled again.

THE EMPEROR'S NEW CLOTHES

I.

ONCE UPON A TIME, in a faraway land, lived a young man called Christian who served in the palace of a wealthy emperor, enjoying the privileges of court life. Christian valued his place at court, for he'd once been very poor and knew the terrible feeling of cold when one didn't have enough clothes, and hunger when there wasn't enough food.

Some years earlier, when Christian had been a young boy, he and his shepherd father had been tending their flock in the hills outside the palace walls when they'd come across a boy, around the same age as Christian, encircled by wolves.

Unbeknown to them, this boy was the Emperor's son, and he'd disobediently left the palace without his guard, chasing

a beautiful peacock. Enchanted by the colourful plumage, the boy was deaf to the hungry wolves' howls. Christian watched in awe as his father approached the snarling wolves, enduring their savage scratches as he beat them away from the boy, lunging at them with his crook. 'No!' yelled the father with a final lunge at the last wolf. As the wolf retreated, the young boy looked up as if awoken from a trance, only at that moment seeing the danger he'd been in.

'Thank you,' he said.

Christian asked, 'Why did you risk your life, Father? You don't know that boy.'

'We are shepherds, my son — protectors,' replied his father. 'We should do what's right, even if it's dangerous.'

The Emperor was so grateful for the safe return of his son that he rewarded Christian's father, who became the young prince's Royal Protector. Christian became his Royal Companion. The two boys grew up together, playing as friends, although Christian knew his place with this boy who would become Emperor.

As they got older, Christian became very good at entertaining, and the prince became very good at being entertained.

When both their fathers died, the prince became the Emperor and Christian became the Royal Protector. Secretly, both young men worried that they wouldn't fill their fathers' shoes. Christian worked hard to become strong and fit, so he'd be ready should there be an attack on the Emperor. Meanwhile the Emperor worked hard to ensure he looked like an emperor – for sadly, too easily enchanted by beautiful gifts and the flattery of the courtiers, he'd grown into a vain young man. He loved clothes and would spend hours dressing to impress, in suits made from only the finest, the rarest, the most exquisitely coloured fabrics the royal suit-makers could find.

The Emperor had suits made for every occasion and every imperial task. He had suits for eating breakfast, suits for riding, suits for playing croquet, suits for listening to amusing stories (which Christian was very good at telling),

suits for feeding the imperial peacocks, even suits for inspecting the royal suit collection. Indeed, the young Emperor spent much time planning his next suit and little time planning for the care of his subjects and kingdom. Christian attended to the Emperor during all his activities. A gifted sportsman and a charming and good-humoured companion, he was a much-liked member of the court. 'That Christian,' the other courtiers would say, 'you can count on him to brighten things up. Always ready with a story, guaranteed to put a smile on the Emperor's face!'

One day Christian and the Emperor were out riding in the hills (the Emperor wearing a jaunty golden suit with small horseshoe motifs embroidered in fine silken thread at the cuffs) when they rode past some villagers collecting juniper berries. The Emperor, who had little contact with life outside the palace walls, was taken aback by their appearance.

'Why are their clothes so dirty?' he exclaimed. 'And why such drab colours?'

'They'll only have one set of clothes each,' explained Christian, who sometimes wished his emperor would spend a little more time out in his kingdom.

'Well, that's ridiculous!' declared the Emperor.

'Perhaps if the Royal Treasury helped the villagers more, Your Highness ...' offered Christian.

'Oh, don't bore me. You're supposed to protect me from such things. Come, Christian, let's away. I need to change into my luncheon suit.'

Christian sighed as he turned his horse back towards the palace. But it wasn't his place to instruct the Emperor, and he didn't want to upset anyone – he loved his life at the palace, and he wanted to keep things that way. He knew the Emperor was a little vain but, Christian reasoned, he was still growing into his job. Christian wanted to protect the Emperor, just like his father had – but he had yet to learn that wolves didn't always look like wolves.

2.

ONE DAY, as the Emperor sat on his throne wearing his throne-sitting suit, the Prime Minister suggested an imperial tour of the villages beyond the palace. The villagers were starting to grumble that the new Emperor cared only for palace life and not for them. The visit would show them the Emperor was a caring leader.

The Emperor leapt at the idea – sadly for the wrong reasons. 'Indeed!' he cried, clapping his hands. 'I must have a kingdom-touring suit made! Call for the finest fabrics!'

The royal call went out and was heard by two swindlers passing through the kingdom. They came to the court and were presented to the Emperor.

Christian watched them bow a little too low before the throne.

'Your Royal Highness,' they said together, 'we offer our services as weavers and tailors, of the finest of cloths, in the most exquisite of colours … and with an extra, *special* quality – a divining quality, if you will.'

That got the Emperor's attention. 'What kind of divining quality?' he asked, leaning closer.

'The best sort, sire,' said one of the swindlers. 'Our fabrics are able to be seen only by people of wisdom. Anyone stupid and unfit to hold their office will be unable to see the cloth, and the suit from which it is made. An invaluable thing for an emperor, don't you agree?'

The Emperor did agree, as the swindlers knew he would. Their plan was devious but quite ingenious: they knew everyone would claim they could see the cloth, to protect their reputations and positions. The swindlers could collect a rich payment in gold by simply pretending to weave a cloth and make a suit that never existed.

'Imagine, sire!' said the other swindler. 'Not only will you look magnificent, but you'll know who is stupid and who is wise. And no one in the world but you will have such a suit.'

Christian wondered how such a thing could be possible, but the Emperor was, again, enchanted. 'I must have this suit!' he declared.

'It will not come cheap, though, sire,' warned the swindlers. 'It will take much gold and many reels of fine silks.'

'Pay these weavers what they ask,' the Emperor instructed the Royal Treasurer. 'Give them whatever they request, and have them start immediately.'

The treasurer looked hesitant but gave the devious weavers a loom, a sewing machine and reels of precious threads, and they set upon their task with zeal.

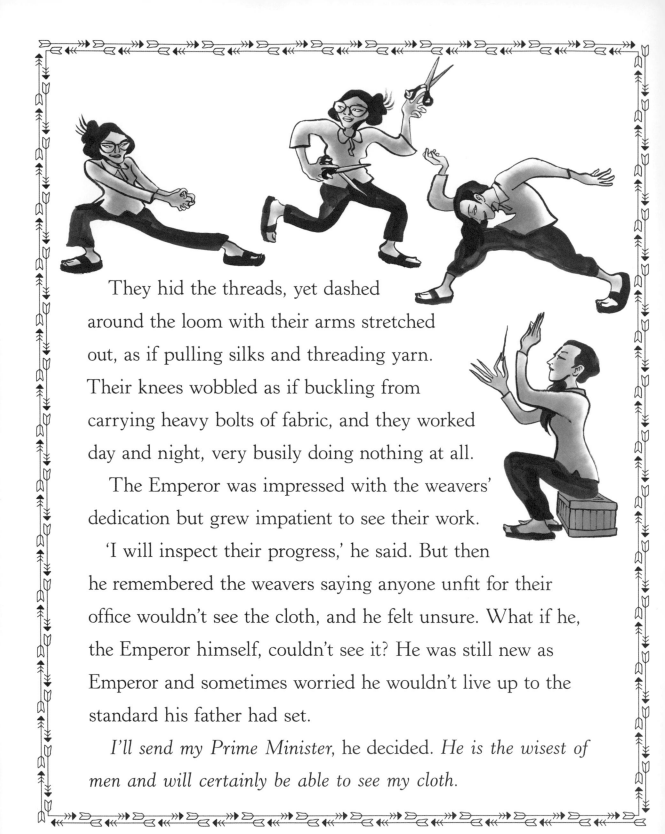

They hid the threads, yet dashed
around the loom with their arms stretched
out, as if pulling silks and threading yarn.
Their knees wobbled as if buckling from
carrying heavy bolts of fabric, and they worked
day and night, very busily doing nothing at all.

The Emperor was impressed with the weavers'
dedication but grew impatient to see their work.

'I will inspect their progress,' he said. But then
he remembered the weavers saying anyone unfit for their
office wouldn't see the cloth, and he felt unsure. What if he,
the Emperor himself, couldn't see it? He was still new as
Emperor and sometimes worried he wouldn't live up to the
standard his father had set.

I'll send my Prime Minister, he decided. *He is the wisest of
men and will certainly be able to see my cloth.*

And so the Prime Minister was summoned. 'Visit the weavers,' the Emperor instructed. 'I should like to know how they're getting on.'

'Yes, Your Highness,' said the Prime Minister, although he too was a little fearful he might not see anything. And, indeed, when he walked into the room, he saw the two weavers busily rushing around but couldn't see a thread of cloth. It was as if the swindlers were working on a completely empty loom – which, indeed, they were. *Oh my*, he thought to himself, *I cannot see a thing.*

The swindlers, sensing the Prime Minister's reluctance, approached him, bowing low.

'What do you think, Prime Minister?' one asked. 'Will the Emperor appreciate this exquisite pattern? Do you not think the colours will match his royal complexion perfectly?'

The Prime Minister cocked his head one way, then the other. He squinted and strained his eyes, but he could see nothing.

'Tell us, Prime Minister,' said the other swindler. 'For surely you can see it? Surely you, the Emperor's most trusted minister, can see our work?'

But the Prime Minister could not.

Am I stupid? he thought. *I wouldn't have thought it so. This mustn't be known – I cannot lose my position.*

And so he cleared his throat and declared the cloth the most beautiful and intricately woven he'd ever seen.

'What do you think will please the Emperor about it most?' pressed the swindlers.

The Prime Minister coughed. 'The brilliant gold trim,' he declared, looking out the window.

'Oh, yes, an excellent choice. What taste and discrimination you have,' they replied. 'And please, wise Prime Minister, order us more silk and gold thread so we can make it even more beautiful.'

The Prime Minister had no choice but to comply. He left the room and reported to the Emperor that the weavers were making a cloth of unimaginable beauty.

A few days later, the Emperor sent his Royal Treasurer to ask when the suit would be ready. Like the Prime Minister, the Treasurer could see nothing on the swindlers' loom, but was too afraid to say so.

The Prime Minister could see it, she thought, *yet I cannot. I must be unfit for office, but I have six children to feed and mustn't lose my position at court.*

And so the Royal Treasurer also declared the cloth the finest she'd seen. 'The Prime Minister didn't adequately convey the beauty!' she exclaimed. 'The vibrancy, the richness!'

'We're so pleased you like it,' said one of the swindlers, barely able to conceal a smirk. 'Which aspect do you think will most enchant His Royal Highness?'

'Ah, well … I'd say the intricate images – the ah, er …'

'Yes, Royal Treasurer, which image?'

Do you mean the peacock?' asked the other swindler, gesturing to the empty space in the middle of the loom.

'Ah, yes! The peacock, the Emperor's favourite bird! And with such detailing. Exquisite!'

The Royal Treasurer reported that the cloth was indeed magnificent, and soon everyone at court was talking about how grand the Emperor's new clothes were going to be.

The Emperor could think of nothing else. 'Tell me again, Prime Minister, about my new suit,' he said the next day in the throne room. He was wearing his black-and-white chequered suit, as he and Christian were playing a game of chess. 'Oh, the silver—' began the Prime Minister. 'I thought you said it was gold,' said Christian.

'Did I say silver? I meant gold. The most luminous gold!' exclaimed the Prime Minister, a little too enthusiastically.

'And the eagle!' added the Royal Treasurer.

'Not peacock?' asked the Emperor. 'I thought you said peacock.'

'Yes, quite right,' said the Royal Treasurer quickly. 'A magnificent peacock.'

'Christian,' said the Emperor, feeling a little impatient with his ministers, 'will you please go and inspect my suit?'

'Of course, sire,' replied Christian. He bowed to the Emperor and left for the weaving room.

When he arrived, as had happened with the Prime Minister and Royal Treasurer before him, Christian saw nothing on the loom. He watched as the two devious weavers rushed around, gesturing frantically at thin air.

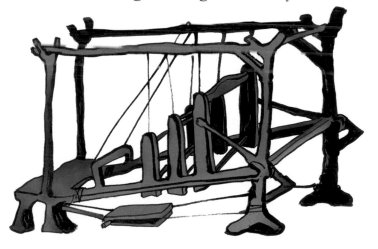

Panicking a little, Christian went closer. *Is there something I can't see?* he asked himself. *Could the fabric truly have powers to tell the wise from the stupid?* He stepped closer still.

'No further, please,' cried one of the weavers. 'The fabric is quite fragile.'

But Christian ignored her, waving his arms up and down in the centre of the loom. He felt nothing.

There is *nothing here,* Christian thought. *I'm sure of it. No gold or silver, no peacock or eagle.* He looked and looked again, until he could look no more, for indeed there was nothing to look at!

'What do you think?' asked one of the weavers, her voice

wavering. 'What part of the Emperor's new cloth do you admire the most?'

Christian said nothing.

'You can see it, can't you?' said the other swindler. 'It is true, of course, that the cloth cannot be seen by stupid people, but surely you, sir, the Emperor's Royal Protector, can see it?'

Christian left the room without a word.

These people are tricksters, he said to himself. *But why did the Prime Minister and Royal Treasurer say they saw something?* Then Christian had a terrible thought. *What will happen if the Emperor falls for this trick too? What if he goes out into the villages wearing only his underwear?*

Christian imagined the royal procession: the trumpeters and banner-bearers marching in front; the royal guards in their uniforms bringing up the rear; and, in the middle, the Emperor, centre of attention, wearing only his underpants.

He'd look ridiculous, Christian realised. *He'd die of embarrassment! Everyone would laugh. But the Prime Minister and Royal Treasurer must have told him they could see the suit so no one would think them stupid.*

Then Christian had another terrible thought, this time for himself.

If I tell the Emperor the truth, perhaps everyone will think I'm stupid. Maybe no one will believe me over the Prime Minister and Royal Treasurer. And what will they do? They might call me a liar, to protect themselves; they could even have me thrown into the royal dungeon!

Maybe, he reasoned, *it's best for me to say nothing, keep out of the way. It's not really my responsibility.* But that didn't feel good to him either. Something about it niggled at his head and his heart. Christian could almost hear his father's voice echo through his mind: *Do what's right.* But Christian, like the Prime Minister and the Royal Treasurer, was afraid he'd lose everything if he did.

3.

CHRISTIAN AVOIDED THE EMPEROR, and to his relief, the very next day, the weavers announced the suit was ready for the Emperor's approval.

Now it's up to him, Christian thought. *He's the Emperor. Surely he'll see there's nothing there and not be afraid to say it.*

The Emperor entered the weaving room, flanked by attendants and courtiers.

'Your Royal Highness,' said the weavers, swooping down into the lowest of bows. 'We are honoured. Tell us, sire, how do you like your royal suit, on which we have laboured these past days and nights?'

'Is it not magnificent?' said the Prime Minister.

'Is it not perfect?' said the Royal Treasurer.

All the other attendants were squinting. The weavers waltzed around the room. 'Do you all see?' they cried. 'Surely, Your Highness, you have no idiots in your court!'

With that, all those other attendants of the court began to exclaim how beautiful they found the cloth.

'Exquisite!'

'The detail!'

'The colours!'

No one would admit they could see nothing at all. Christian's heart sank. He turned to the Emperor. 'Sire, what do you see?'

I see nothing, thought the Emperor. *Not one thread. Am I unfit to be Emperor? Everyone will realise I can't live up to my father.*

The Emperor didn't look at Christian. Instead, he turned
to the weavers. 'Magnificent,' he declared. 'I'll wear it
tomorrow.'

'But Your Highness– ' Christian started.

'Can you not see the suit?' asked one of the swindlers
sharply.

'Well, boy?' snapped the Prime Minister, who'd always
been a bit jealous of Christian's closeness to the Emperor.
'Can you? To the dungeon with you if you can't, for that
surely means you're unfit to serve our Royal Emperor.'

Christian was silent. He wanted to say something, but
nothing came out.

The Prime Minister gave a scoffing laugh and ordered the
weavers to have the suit completed by morning for the tour.

The Emperor glanced at Christian, but then turned towards his attendants, who were encircling him now, crooning, congratulating him on his splendid new suit. Christian left the room unnoticed.

What do I do? he asked himself. *I'm just one voice. Everyone's saying they can see beautiful cloth, but there's nothing there, I know it. And if the Emperor insists on wearing this nothing, he'll walk out of the palace gates tomorrow in only his underwear and be eaten alive by the mocking crowd.*

Christian thought of his father again and realised there was only one thing to do – he had to speak up, even it meant risking his popularity and comfortable life at the palace. It was his turn to save the Emperor.

4.

THE NEXT MORNING the weavers declared the suit ready and the Emperor, attended by the Royal Dresser, entered the weaving room. Some time later he came out wearing only his underpants: large, baggy blue-and-white-striped bloomers.

He looks ridiculous! thought Christian. *Why is he doing this? He's the Emperor – surely he's not afraid of what others might think?*

The attendants, the guards, the trumpeters and the banner-bearers were all staring at the Emperor. First there was silence. Then, as they realised their jobs would be in danger if they laughed, all began to cheer: 'Bravo, Your Majesty, bravo!'

'This is crazy,' said Christian, and he moved towards the Emperor.

The Prime Minister, who'd heard him, blocked his path. 'Anyone who doesn't agree the Emperor looks the finest he's ever looked will be thrown into the royal dungeon,' he stated.

Christian's heart raced, but he knew what he had to do. 'Stop!' he cried. Everyone looked at him. 'Sire, there is no suit. You're wearing only your underwear, and if you—'

'Hah!' shouted the Prime Minister furiously. 'The shepherd boy can't see the suit. He's unfit. I always thought so. Trust me, sire!'

Christian looked imploringly at the Emperor. 'Sire, don't go out of the palace grounds like this. Your subjects will surely laugh at you.'

The Emperor looked at Christian, then down at himself.
He seemed not to see his skinny legs poking out from his
blue-and-white-striped underpants.

'Sire,' said the Royal Treasurer, terrified now that the
Emperor would know she'd lied,
'trust us, not this shepherd boy.'

'Guards,' cried the Prime
Minister, pointing at Christian,
'take him to the dungeon.
He is stripped of all title and
privileges.'

Two guards roughly took hold of Christian, who watched
helplessly as the near-naked Emperor walked towards the

huge palace gates, which were being
slowly wound open. Once the gates
had fully opened, all the villagers
beyond would see him.
There was no time to lose.
With a roar, Christian broke free
of the guards. He ripped the
Prime Minister's cape from
his shoulders and rushed

towards the Emperor, shouting, 'No!' as he lunged and covered him with it just seconds before the gates opened wide.

The Emperor looked at Christian as if awoken from a trance, only at that moment seeing the danger he'd been in.

'Christian,' he said, 'I'm in my underpants! The people could have seen me like this. Me, the Emperor! You've saved me from such embarrassment!'

'It was my pleasure, your Royal Highness,' replied Christian.

In gratitude for his boldness and courage, the Emperor declared that Christian would now be both Royal Protector and Advisor. He then glared at the Prime Minister and Royal Treasurer who, quite sensibly, looked very worried.

The hidden spools of thread were discovered, and the swindlers were caught and thrown into the royal dungeon. The Prime Minister and Royal Treasurer now had to seek Christian's approval on all matters of court. And the first matter was the distribution of many of the Emperor's old clothes throughout the kingdom.

And they all – well, mostly all – lived happily ever after.

PRINCE LEO AND THE SLEEPING PRINCESS

1.

ONCE UPON A TIME, in a faraway kingdom, lived a young prince. Prince Leopold Charming, Leo to his friends, was a prince from a long line of princes who, throughout the centuries, had fulfilled the Charming family's time-honoured role of rescuing damsels, mostly princesses, in distress.

Leo showed every indication that he would uphold the Charming family tradition brilliantly: he was strong and athletic, an expert horseman and archer, and a quite superb fencer, and he practised all with great diligence. He was less interested in ballroom dancing, which was often part of the post-rescue work, but as he was an obedient boy he persevered with his waltz and was, according to the Royal Dance Master, really quite good, with a strong sense of rhythm. Leo was also a disciplined student of princely history, reading the Charming Family Chronicles and learning from both the triumphs and travails of his ancestors' rescues.

The great hall of Charming Castle was filled with paintings in heavy gold frames displaying family portraits of princes and the princesses they had rescued and married: Leo's parents, grandparents, great-grandparents, great-great-grandparents and even-greater-grandparents. Leo didn't mind

princesses – he knew quite a few nice ones – but he didn't want to get married, at least not now, at least not for ages. For Leo had a lot to do. He played the violin, both alone and with his friends, and he was particularly good at royal tennis: his princely brain was highly mathematical, and he loved to calculate exactly where the ball would land if he hit it at a certain angle and speed. Leo couldn't spend as much time as he'd like playing, though, for he had his daily fencing and archery practice, his tower-scaling and castle-entwining-briar-beating and, most importantly, his dragon-slaying drills to complete.

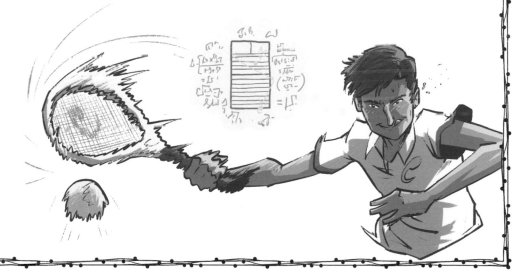

Leo didn't mind all the training – he understood it was his duty – but he did sometimes wonder why damsel deliverance always came down to the princes. His closest friends, the Honourable Viscounts Edvard and Gilbert, would both make admirable defenders, but they were never called – it was always the princes. And, Leo wondered, what about the princesses? Could they not ever rescue themselves?

Leo raised this with his father one day as they walked in the royal gardens training their falcons, their dogs obediently by their sides.

'Now there's a thought,' said King Oskar, pondering the question as he tethered the peregrine falcon that had just returned to his arm. 'Do you know, Leo, I've never thought of that – it's never come up. I like your thinking, though.'

That made Leo smile: he liked to make his father happy.

'I suppose it's about our role,' continued the King. 'The viscounts – and those dukes and marquises – all have their roles to play, and we ours. We have this wonderful palace, these beautiful gardens…'

'And the royal tennis court,' chipped in Leo.

'Indeed,' said his father, smiling, for the King knew how much his son loved his royal tennis. 'And with those privileges come responsibilities. Our responsibility is to serve when needed, by rescuing – it's what we do, and we must ensure we do it well. Let's walk some more, Leo.'

The King and the prince walked down the ordered paths of the palace's highly ornamental parterre gardens: straight gravel-filled paths separated by square garden beds, all exactly the same size and bordered by green box-hedging, bursting with snowdrops, hyacinths, geraniums, lavender, and precisely placed and masterfully pruned rose bushes. The garden had been first planned and planted by Leo's great-great-great-grandfather and grandmother and had been immaculately maintained ever since. In the exact centre was a pond, and in the middle of the pond was an imposing bronze statue of Prince Leo's great-great-great-grandfather, slaying a dragon.

While Leo loved a fast gallop in the woods outside the palace walls, rushing at breakneck speed, he also loved walking in the palace gardens. It made him feel calm and secure – as if things were under control, at peace. It was a good place for thinking, his father often said, which was why he would often walk there with Leo to instruct him in the Charming family ways. And so it was this day, when the King told Leo the legend of the sleeping princess.

2.

'LEGEND HAS IT,' began the King, 'that there was once a small kingdom neighbouring ours ruled by a gracious king and queen who, after many years of waiting and wishing, had a daughter, whom they named Aurora.

There was much rejoicing throughout the land, and in honour of the Princess Aurora's christening, a royal banquet was held. The King and Queen invited all the fairies in the kingdom except one, an evil fairy, for they feared she would ruin the celebration.'

'Why do I get the feeling that wasn't a good idea?' asked Leo.

'Quite,' said the King. 'And, indeed, when all but one of the good fairies had bestowed their blessings on the little

princess, a black raven flew through the palace window and transformed into the evil fairy. Outraged that she'd been excluded, she put a curse on the princess, declaring that when she was sixteen years of age, she would prick her finger on a spindle and die.'

'Prick her finger? That's a bit lame, isn't it, Father?' asked Leo.

'Well, fairies do as fairies do, I suppose,' said the King. 'Shall I continue?'

'Yes, Father,' said Prince Leo, although he wasn't completely sure what this story had to do with him.

'The Queen and King were devastated they would soon lose their so-longed-for daughter. There was, however, one fairy left to bestow a final blessing, and while she couldn't cancel the evil fairy's curse—'

'Why not?' asked Leo.

'Well, because once some things are said, they can't be unsaid,' replied the King, 'but the last fairy could soften the curse so the princess wouldn't die, but rather would fall into a deep sleep. The good fairy pronounced her blessing, and the evil fairy hissed, transformed into a snake and slipped out of the palace before anyone could catch her. The King ordered every spindle in the land to be burnt. He made it a crime punishable by death to spin anything anywhere in the kingdom, yet somehow, on her sixteenth birthday—'

'Sixteen, same age as me,' said Leo.

'Yes, an important age for princes and princesses,' said the King. 'Well, on her sixteenth birthday, the princess wandered into a room in the castle where an old servant-woman in a black cape was hunched over a spindle, spinning thread through her gnarled fingers. The old woman was—'

'I know!' shouted Leo, for he was well-versed in the ways of evil fairies and goblins. 'The old woman was the evil fairy in disguise!'

'Yes,' said the King, looking proud. 'Well done, Leo.'

Leo beamed as his father continued.

'The old woman beckoned to Princess Aurora. "Come in, my dear. Let me show you the fine gold thread I'm spinning," she croaked. The princess, who'd of course never seen a spindle before, was entranced. The woman handed her the spindle, on which Aurora pricked her finger. In that instant, she fell to the ground.'

'But not dead, right?' said Leo.

'Just sleeping, because of the good fairy's counter-blessing?'

'Exactly,' said King Oskar. 'Seconds later, a chambermaid walked in and found the princess lying on the floor and a large black spider scuttling away. She called for the King and Queen, and they called for the court doctors and the good fairies, but no one could wake the princess. The curse had taken hold. Aurora was carried to a room high in a tower and surrounded by garlands of flowers. Her royal flag flew from the tower but, inside, the princess lay completely still.'

'That's sad,' said Leo.

'Yes, terribly,' said the King. 'Everyone was so sad that the King and Queen asked a good fairy to cast a spell of sleep over the whole castle. Everyone who lived in the castle – the cooks, the servants, the footmen and ladies-in-waiting, knights and ministers and even the King and Queen – all fell into a deep sleep exactly where they were.'

'That's a bit creepy,' said Leo.

'Yes, I suppose it is,' said King Oskar with a shudder. 'The whole castle was now wrapped in timeless sleep. Years went by, and the trees in the grounds grew tall, the bushes thick, the grass high. Thorny briars curled up the walls and turrets. It is said that all this happened over a hundred years ago, and that the forgotten palace sleeps on to this day.'

'Would anything awaken the princess?'

'According to legend, "only the piercing of the evil fairy's heart by a king's son, one young and true, bold and of blood royally blue" can break the spell,' said the King.

Now Leo understood why his father was telling him the story. 'And that's where we come in, isn't it?' said Leo.

'Where you come in, maybe,' replied the King. 'My princess-saving days are over, but this is what you've been training for, Leo. Always take your shield and sword when you ride in the woods, and ride further and deeper in – perhaps you'll find the hidden castle.'

Leo obeyed his father. Every week he'd mount his white stallion and dutifully ride out in the woods, careful to take a different path each time, his sword and shield (royal-blue-coloured, with three gold *fleurs-de-lys*) always with him. But the weeks went by and Leo never saw anything, which was, frankly, disappointing: he'd been excited at the thought of putting his training to the test, but there seemed no princess with whom to do it. He began to think the legend of the sleeping princess was just a story after all.

3.

SOME MONTHS LATER

Leo was dutifully setting off for his
weekly ride into the woods when
Viscount Edvard called, 'Leo, stay
here. Play royal tennis with us instead!'

'I can't,' said Leo, strapping his sword to his
back. 'It's time for my woods ride.'

'But you never find anything, Leo!' said Viscount Gilbert.

It was true: despite his many rides, he never did find
anything. Leo was sorely tempted to stay but he knew his
duty. 'Maybe later,' he said and climbed onto his horse.

'Royal tennis will be more fun,' pleaded Viscount Edvard.
But it was too late: Leo had ridden down the path, out the
royal gates and into the woods.

Heading westward, Leo rode for over an hour through
particularly dense forest before he came to a thick tangle of
thorny briars. 'Just like in the story,' he said to himself.

Right, left, right, left. Leo moved his sword expertly through the tangle of thorns, grateful for all his lessons and arm-strengthening exercises.

Just as he was tiring, his sword ripped through the last cluster and Leo saw what it had been hiding – two gatehouses to the sides of a long and narrow stone bridge, which spanned a deep, tree-filled ravine and led to an imposing castle.

Leo climbed off his horse and led it as he approached the bridge, his whole body tingling with excitement. He slashed at the thorny creepers covering the door of a gatehouse and pushed with all his strength to open it. Inside he found two armour-clad guards, crossbows still in hand, slumped on the floor. He checked their chests. They were still breathing: they were asleep. Leo looked up at the castle. The tallest tower, entwined in brambles, flew a tattered royal flag.

It hadn't been just a story! Leo had found the castle of the sleeping princess.

Leo looked up the castle's wall, calculating the height of the tower. *Shouldn't take too long,* he thought as he approached it and grabbed hold of the thorny branches, his hands protected by his thick riding gloves, then began to climb.

But, as he reached the top, a black raven swooped at him, pecking viciously at his hands. It swooped again and Leo swung at it, using his tennis backhand stroke to send it tumbling away. Leo pulled himself up onto the stone window ledge and looked in. There on a bed, surrounded by dry, dead flowers, was a girl in a blue dress. Leo couldn't help but also notice a cello and a royal tennis racquet leaning against the wall. 'It really is the princess!' he exclaimed. 'How terrible! All the things she could have been doing. I must break the curse.'

Just then the raven returned, pecking at his eyes. Leo swiped at it again, but this time he lost his grip on the brambles and fell from the ledge as the raven

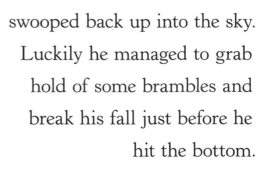

swooped back up into the sky. Luckily he managed to grab hold of some brambles and break his fall just before he hit the bottom.

'That was close!' he said. 'Now I need to find that evil fairy. Perhaps if I can get inside the castle...'

But then there was a ferocious crack of thunder from the sky and, although it was the middle of the day, everything went dark.

Leo's horse whinnied nervously and he jumped onto its back, a tremor of nerves shooting through his body. What would happen next? Leo didn't have to wait long to find out.

'Who dares disturb my accursed castle?' shrieked a voice.

Leo looked up to see a figure, taller than three women and dressed in a swirling purple-and-black winged cape, with a horned crown on her head, standing on top of the castle's highest turret. She held a long sceptre, which she now pointed at Leo.

'The evil fairy. Yes!' said Leo.

The fairy grew taller still, and now there was a flash of

lightning.

The thorny briars
clutching the castle walls
sprang out, as if alive, and curled towards Leo on the
bridge. Leo again took up his sword, and he struck at them
powerfully, sending them flying to either side of him.

The fairy, enraged, raised her sceptre again and sent
showers of fire down onto the bridge, igniting the brambles.
Flames began to lick around Leo's boots but the prince
stood his ground, using his shield to deflect
the fiery darts the evil one rained
down upon him and his horse.
Now the trees in the ravine caught
fire, and the enchantress raised
her sceptre again, unleashing a
lightning bolt that struck the
bridge in front of Leo right

between him and the castle, the stone
crumbling into the flames below.
'You will not proceed!' the enchantress bellowed.
'My curse will stand. You will concede!'
Prince Leo knew he wouldn't concede. Everything
he'd trained for had prepared him for this moment.
'That's not the way we do things in my family,'
he said as he prodded his horse firmly,
backtracked a little and then charged towards
the breach in the bridge. With a flying
leap, he landed on the other side.

The enchantress, incensed, transformed into a huge black-and-purple dragon, spraying a hideous green slime from its mouth and hurling fireballs from its claws. The dragon swept down and landed beside Leo. It belched a torrent of green slime at him, but he used his shield and held strong, deflecting it. The slime hit the castle wall, blasting through the stone.

That was close, thought Leo.

The dragon struck again and again, but each time Leo matched it perfectly, until, repelling a giant fireball and sending it scorching into the dragon, Leo lost his footing. He scrambled up but struggled to get back into position in time to deflect the next slime attack – Leo knew the moment it hit his shield that he'd made a mistake. The shield flew out of his hand.

The dragon moved in. Leo held his sword tight and advanced.

He remembered what his father had told him of the legend: 'Only the piercing of the evil fairy's heart by a king's son, one young and true, bold and of blood royally blue can break the spell.'

I'm a king's son, he told himself. *This is what I need to do, what I have trained for. Pierce the heart, break the curse, and let that princess get on with what she needs to do.*

Leo took a deep breath. He knew he had to get close. He advanced on the dragon, ducking the slime and fireballs, until he was so close he could see its hideous scaly skin. The dragon rose up on its hind legs, exposing its chest.

Now! thought Leo.

He hurled his sword, and it pierced the dragon's heart.

`YEWARRRRRRRRRGGHHHHH!'

The dragon's scream was ear-splitting. It lurched and then fell from the bridge, into the fiery pit below. There was an explosion and then, eerily, nothing. At that moment, the sky became a brilliant blue and the sun shone its rays all over the castle. Leo's sword lay glistening on the bridge by the castle gates, which now opened before him.

Wait until I tell Father about this! Leo thought.

4.

LEO WALKED THROUGH the castle gates just as guards
in the courtyard got up from the ground, stretching. A
doorman held the castle door open for Leo, stifling a yawn,
and inside the great entrance hall servants, footmen and
ladies-in-waiting rose to their feet too, looking bewildered.

'Um, I need to see the princess,' Leo told a young woman
who was rubbing her eyes.

'The princess!' she exclaimed, as if suddenly remembering.
'Have you not heard, sir, that my lady is asleep, victim of the
cruellest of curses? She'll be asleep for years, until a king's
son, someone young—'

She stopped mid-sentence, looking intently at Leo.

'You! Are you the one, who is young and true, bold and of blood royally blue?'

'Well, madam, I am royal,' replied Leo. 'And, if I may say so, I think I have just been pretty bold with a particularly evil fairy.'

'And she is dead?' asked the lady-in-waiting.

'Very much so,' confirmed Leo.

'Then the spell is broken, and Princess Aurora will be awake! Oh my goodness, I must go to her! And the King and Queen!'

The lady-in-waiting turned to a footman. 'Call for the bells to be rung and trumpets sounded. The spell over this castle is broken! And look, on the stairs!'

The lady-in-waiting dropped to the floor in a low curtsey. Leo looked up to the top of the grand staircase to see the princess awake and smiling, standing in between a king and queen (Leo could tell them by their crowns).

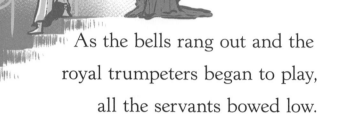

As the bells rang out and the royal trumpeters began to play, all the servants bowed low.

'Your Majesties!' Prince Leo bowed down in front of the King, Queen and Princess Aurora.

'Arise, noble prince,' said the Queen. 'With your courage, you have destroyed the evil fairy and broken the curse. What is your name?'

'Prince Leopold Charming at your service,' replied Leo, grinning.

'We owe you an enormous debt of gratitude,' said the Queen. 'I could kiss you, I'm so happy! May I?'

'Of course,' replied Leo happily, 'but you don't owe me anything, Your Majesty. It's my job.'

'Well, we can still say thank you!' said Princess Aurora, descending the stairs. 'I can't tell you how happy I am to be awake. I have a lot to do! I can get on with my archery and—'

'Archery?' asked Leo. He wasn't expecting that.

'Oh yes,' said the King, looking proudly at his daughter. 'Aurora has a great eye. She's quite the expert markswoman.'

'And then there's her tennis,' said the Queen. 'That volley! Ah, and now you'll play again, my dear girl.'

'I adore tennis,' said Leo. 'We have a really good court at our castle. I play with my two best friends, Edvard and Gilbert, and we'd love another player for doubles. You could come over and play with us one day, if you'd like?'

'I'd be thrilled to,' said Aurora. 'I'm a little out of practice, though.'

Leo grinned. 'That will make you easier to beat.'

'Not that out of practice,' replied Aurora quickly.

'You're on!' said Leo.

Over the next weeks and months, Leo and Aurora spent a lot of time together, playing in their newly formed string quartet with Gilbert and Edvard or on the royal tennis court where Gilbert and Edvard always wanted to pair up with Aurora, for she was by far the strongest player.

But Leo always had Aurora as his partner.

'After all, guys,' said Aurora, 'it was Leo who did the dragon-slaying and curse-breaking.'

'Quite true,' said Edvard.

'Fair point,' conceded Gilbert.

And so, more often than not, Leo and Aurora thrashed the viscounts, and they all lived happily ever after.